DISNEY · PIXAR

Rex to the Rescue!

Adapted from the film by Justine and Ron Fontes

DISNEY
PRESS

New York

Printed in the United States of America.
First Edition
1 3 5 7 9 10 8 6 4 2
Library of Congress Catalog Card Number:
ISBN: 0-7868-4288-1
This book was set in 16-point Berkeley Book.

For more Disney Press fun, visit www.DisneyBooks.com.

Chapter One

The High Shelf

RROOAAWWRR! Did I scare you?
Heh-heh. Don't worry. It's just me—Rex.
Sure I'm a Tyrannosaurus, one of the biggest,
baddest dinosaurs ever. But I'm really just
a toy. All of us, me and Woody the cowboy,
Hamm the piggy bank, Mr. Potato Head,
Buzz Lightyear, and the rest of the toys,
belong to a boy named Andy Davis.

My pal Buzz and I were playing the "Buzz

1

Lightyear" video game. I lost the game, as usual.

"I'm never gonna defeat Zurg!" I groaned. "I give up!"

"Pull yourself together," Buzz replied calmly. "Remember, a Space Ranger must turn and face his fears no matter how ugly it gets. You must not flinch."

Buzz's pep talk made me want to tackle the evil Zurg right now! But Woody needed Buzz's attention.

Woody was excited about going to cowboy camp with Andy. Buzz would be in charge with Woody gone. Woody rubbed his head as he read his long list.

"Woody, you haven't found your hat yet, have you?" Buzz asked.

"No! Andy's leaving any minute and I can't find it anywhere," Woody said.

While Bo Peep kissed Woody good-bye,

her sheep grabbed the cord of my game control and started chewing! I didn't want to mess with them. Sheep can be surprisingly mean. Besides, there were three of them. I said, "Miss Peep, your sheep . . ."

Bo whistled and the sheep suddenly let go. I flopped over and fell on the TV's remote control, accidentally turning it on. A noisy commercial popped on the screen.

"Moooooo! Hey, kids! This is Al from Al's Toy Barn!"

A man in a chicken suit chattered and clucked a mile a minute about the good deals at his store.

"Turn it off!" Woody cried. "Someone's going to hear!"

"Which button is *off*?!" I pushed buttons frantically as Al chattered on. "So hurry on down to Al's Toy Barn. Just get off on highway . . ."

"Oh, let me," Hamm grunted. He pushed a button and the TV went black.

BARK! BARK! BARK! Dog claws clattered in the hallway. Andy's puppy suddenly burst into the room!

"Ahh! It's Buster!" I cried, shaking from head to tail.

The big, scary wiener dog was Andy's Christmas present last year. He looked like Slinky, only without the spring. But what a monster! Huge teeth flashed in his slobbery mouth.

Bo Peep called from her tabletop, "Woody, hide, quick!"

Woody ran into hiding. But the monster

4

dog had his scent and pulled Woody from Andy's duffel bag. The monster stood over Woody and licked him. Yuck!

Suddenly, we heard voices beyond the door. Andy was coming in to get his stuff! We all raced back to where he had left us.

Andy picked us up and started playing. He had time for one more game before he left for camp.

He worked Woody's and Buzz's hands to make them perform their secret handshake . . . *RRRRRIP!* Woody's arm ripped!

Andy was very upset. His mom suggested that they fix him on the way.

"No, just leave him," Andy said reluctantly.

"I'm sorry, honey, but you know, toys don't last forever." Mrs. Davis sighed. She put Woody on the highest shelf in the room, and left with Andy.

"What happened?" I asked.

Mr. Potato Head was shocked. "Woody's been shelved!"

Woody watched as the car pulled away. "Andy!" he gasped. Then he slumped back on the shelf.

Chapter Two

Yard Sale of Doom

Woody wasn't alone on the dusty shelf. Among the books was Wheezy the Penguin, an old squeak toy who had lost his squeaker.

Wheezy pointed out the window. Mrs. Davis was having a yard sale! Yard sales are really scary—Toys who go to yard sales never come back.

Buzz's emergency roll call made sure we were all still in Andy's room. We were, down to the last Green Army Man. But then

I heard footsteps in the hall. Everyone ran to their positions and froze. Mrs. Davis came in with a box marked **25 cents**. She reached under the bed where Slinky hid. I couldn't look! But she didn't take the plastic dog, just an old pair of Velcro sneakers. Then she reached for me! Mrs. Davis put me on top of the table and picked up the worn-out puzzle I'd been lying on. What a relief!

But then Mrs. Davis walked to the shelf and reached up. She got down some old books and then . . . Wheezy!

Woody panicked. He cares about every one of Andy's toys, even old Wheezy. After Mrs. Davis left, Woody struggled with his lame arm. He managed to lift his fingers to his lips and choke out a whistle.

Buster skittered into Andy's room!

"Here, Buster! Here, boy!" Woody called.

He lowered himself off the shelf. He slipped and fell—oh, no!

Luckily, Woody landed on Buster's back. He sat up on the dog like a cowboy on a horse. "Okay, boy, to the yard sale!" Woody commanded. "Yaw!"

"Don't do it, Woody, we love you!" I exclaimed.

Woody galloped downstairs. We all gathered at the window to see what would happen. Buzz looked through Lenny the binoculars.

"Is Woody out there?" I looked over Buzz's shoulder. Woody had jumped on a table and climbed into the **25 cents** box!

Hamm cried, "He's selling himself cheap!"

"Hold on, he's got something," Buzz reported. "It's Wheezy!"

Woody got Wheezy out of the box and pushed the plastic penguin under Buster's

collar. Then Woody climbed back on the dog.

"Way to go, cowboy!" Buzz cheered.

"Yay, Woody!" I cried.

But before they could get back to the house, Buster jumped over a skateboard and Woody fell off!

Buster ran into the house and a little girl picked up the fallen sheriff.

"Hey, that's not her toy!" I said.

I felt better when the girl's mommy put Woody on a table. But then a funny-looking man picked up the cowboy. He excitedly examined Woody. And he got even more excited when he found his hat in the grass.

She told the man Woody was not for sale. The man waved lots of money in her face. But Andy's mom refused to sell Woody. She locked him in her metal cash box.

"That was close," Mr. Potato Head observed. "Go home, Mr. Fancy Car," he added. But the man didn't leave. He kicked the skateboard into some of the sale items to distract Andy's mom. And while Mrs. Davis picked up the scattered stuff, the man pried open the cash box!

"Oh, no! He's stealing Woody!" Buzz said.

"That's illegal!" I said. "Somebody do something!"

The man locked Woody in the trunk of his fancy car and sped off.

Woody was gone!

Chapter Three

Through Darkest Night

LZTYBRN.

That's what Buzz read on the license plate of the toynapper's car.

"There's some sort of message encoded on that vehicle's ID tag," Buzz insisted.

"LAZY TOY BRAIN," Mr. Spell droned in his mechanical voice. "LIZ TRY BRAN. LIZ TAYLOR BRIAN."

Suddenly Buzz punched letters into Mr. Spell.

"AL'S TOY BARN," Mr. Spell announced.

"Al's Toy Barn?" Mr. Potato Head, Bo, and I cried at once.

"Etch, draw that man in the chicken suit!" Buzz commanded. The image appeared on Etch's screen.

"It *is* the chicken man!" I exclaimed.

We had our first clue, but we were a long way from rescuing Woody. We had to find Al's Toy Barn.

I flipped through TV channels, trying to find the commercial for Al's Toy Barn. "Al doesn't seem to be on any of these channels."

"Keep looking," Buzz said.

Hamm bumped me aside and began flicking the channels faster than I could see. Suddenly, there was the chicken man!

"Stop! There it is!" I cried.

Hamm flipped back to the channel in time for us all to hear, "Just get off on Highway Twenty-one and look for the giant chicken." Then a map flashed on the TV screen.

"Now, Etch!" Buzz commanded. Etch copied the map.

"That's where I need to go!" Buzz said, pointing at the X in the center of the

map.

"You can't go, Buzz!" I cried. "You'll never make it!"

But Buzz was already copying the map from Etch's screen to a piece of paper. "Woody once risked his life to save me. I couldn't call myself his friend if I didn't do the  same. So who's with me?"

The next thing I knew we were all standing on the roof of Andy's house.

Suddenly, Mr. Potato Head grabbed Slinky's back end and jumped off the roof!

What had I gotten myself into? Hamm jumped next. Then it was my turn. I tried to feel like a Space Ranger, but my feet didn't want to move.

JA-SWING! I bounced to the ground, then back up to the roof.

"The idea is to let go!" Slinky barked. He was upside down. No, I was upside down! *SWA-IIING!* I let go and landed with a thump.

15

I'd never been on a rescue mission before. I tried to remember all I could from the Buzz Lightyear video game and playing with Andy.

Buzz checked the map. "Good work, men. One block down and only nineteen more to go."

"My parts are killing me!" Mr. Potato Head complained.

"Come on, fellas," Buzz said. "Did Woody give up when Sid had me strapped to a rocket?

"We have a friend in need and until he's safe in Andy's room we will not rest," Buzz declared. "Now, let's move out!"

So we kept walking. Finally, as the sun rose the next morning, Hamm exclaimed, "Hey, guys! Why did the toys cross the road?"

"Oooh! Why?" I asked.

"To get to the chicken ON THE OTHER

SIDE!" Hamm pointed one of his black trotters across the street. The giant chicken! We had found Al's Toy Barn!

"Hurray! The chicken!" I roared.

Then I realized we had a big, busy, two-lane problem. Horns blared. A giant truck rumbled past us. Its huge tires sent a crushed soda can flipping toward us like a Frisbee.

"We'll have to cross," Buzz said.

"I may not be a smart dog, but I know what roadkill is," Slinky added.

But Buzz wouldn't give up. "There must be a safe way . . ." he mused. Then he spotted some orange traffic cones and said, "Okay, here's our chance!" Horns

honked all around us and brakes squealed,
but somehow we safely made it across the
road by hiding under the traffic cones.

Behind us was the biggest traffic jam ever!
But we didn't care.

"Good job, troops. We're that much closer
to Woody," Buzz said.

Chapter Four

To Al's Toy Barn—
and Beyond!

We made it! Everyone jumped on the
mat, trying to get the doors to open. I

marched onto the mat, too. But nothing happened.

Buzz realized what was wrong. "All together!" he said. And on his count, we jumped. *WHOOOSH!* The doors to Al's Toy Barn opened. It was enormous.

"Whoaa, Nellie. How're we gonna find Woody in this place?" Slinky drawled."Look for Al. We find Al, we find Woody," Buzz declared. "Now, move out!"

I followed Mr. Potato Head down an aisle. There I found the answer to all my problems: a *Defeat Zurg* book! At last I'd be able to win! Suddenly a red race car came skidding down the aisle straight for us!

The car screeched to a halt. "I thought we could search in style," Hamm said from the driver's seat.

While we rode around, I read more from the *Defeat Zurg* manual. I didn't mean to, but I got the book in everyone's faces and the car swerved wildly.

"Rex! Watch it!" everyone yelled. "We can't see!" The car skidded out of control.

The Zurg manual flew out of my tiny hands. "My source of power!" I jumped out of the car and fell flat on my face. "Where'd it go?" I looked back and saw the others speeding down the aisle. "Wait! Dinosaur overboard!" I ran after the car.

The car suddenly stopped and I slammed into it headfirst. Ow!

We turned down the Buzz Lightyear aisle.

"Hey, Buzz!" Hamm shouted.

Buzz turned and fired his laser at us! "Halt! Who goes there?"

Mr. Potato Head scolded Buzz. "Quit clowning around and get in the car."

"Buzz! Buzz!" I said excitedly. "I know how to defeat Zurg! I'll tell you on the way,"

I said. Buzz jumped in the car.

While the others searched, I told the Space Ranger. "The secret entrance to Zurg's fortress is to the left, hidden in the shadows."

"To the left and in the shadows," Buzz repeated. "Got it."

Then we heard Al arrive at the store. He was talking on his cell phone.

"Everyone take cover!" Buzz commanded.

We all hid under Al's desk. He flipped switches and turned on machines, all the while talking about some big deal. He set a bag down on the floor beside the desk.

Al pushed a photo through his fax machine. The picture fell to the floor in front of us. The picture showed Woody with his arm fixed!

Then I heard him say, "Now that I have your attention, imagine we add another zero to the price, huh?" When he heard the answer, Al jumped up and down and said, "Yes, yes, you've got a deal! I'll be on the next flight to Japan!"

"He's selling Woody to a toy museum!" Mr. Potato Head saw the whole recipe now.

"In Japan!" I cried.

Buzz guided us into Al's bag. "Into the poultry man's cargo unit! He'll lead us to Zurg."

Al laughed and picked up the bag. But he

didn't notice us, even though my tail was
sticking out!

Al was going to take us straight to Woody.
But when we got to the apartment building,
Al left his bag in the car. We were locked in!

Chapter Five

Tower of Terror

"**H**e didn't take the bag!" I yelled.

Buzz hopped over me and jumped out of the bag. "No time to lose!" He pulled on the door handle, but it wouldn't open. Buzz looked out the window. "He's ascending in the vertical transporter."

Buzz leaned against a button. *KA-CHUNK!*
The car lock popped open!

We wasted no time running across the
yard. Buzz read the elevator indicator
through the glass doors. "Blast! He's on
Level Twenty-three."

"Troops! Over here!" Buzz took the cover
off an air vent. He smiled at me. "Just like
you said, Lizardman, Zurg's hideout: in the
shadows, to the left. Okay, let's move."

Lizardman? I'm not a lizard. I'm a
dinosaur!

We scrambled into the clanging air duct.
With a *CLANK* and a grind, machinery
started up.

"We've been detected! The walls are
closing in!" Buzz shouted.

Buzz lifted up Mr. Potato Head. "Quick,
help me prop up Vegetable Man or we're

done for!"

"Put me down, ya hockey puck!" Mr. Potato Head said angrily.

I was looking for the way out and saw what made the noise. "Hey, guys, look! It's not the walls. It's the elevator!"

Buzz carried us up the shiny shaft. Then he got a bright idea. "What was I thinking? My antigravity servos . . ." He pressed a button on his belt. "Hang tight, everyone.

I'm going to let go of the wall. Three . . .
two . . . one . . ."

Buzz pushed off the wall and struck a
flying pose. Didn't he remember he couldn't
fly? We were doomed! We all screamed
and fell . . .

. . . about two inches. We fell right on
top of the rising elevator. Buzz stood on the
top of the car in his flying pose. "To infinity
and beyond!"

We were brought up even with an air
vent. "Okay, troops! The antigravity
sickness will wear off momentarily. Now,
let's move!"

We thumped down another echoing
stretch of duct. Suddenly we heard a voice.
"Please, no more, I'm begging you!"

Slinky sniffed the air. "That's Woody!" he
howled.

"This way!" Buzz charged forward. But

we were stopped by a grate at the end of the duct.

As we ran toward it, the grate shook loose and fell. We ran straight into the room, past a group of toys, and smack into a wall.

We had found Woody. He was with some strange toys.

There was an old Prospector still in his box, a cowgirl with pretty yarn hair, and a horsie. I'm always shy when I meet new toys. These toys looked surprised. "What's going on here?" the Prospector asked.

"Guys! How did you find me?" Woody asked with a big smile.

"We're here to spring you," Slinky said.

We swarmed the strangers. Hamm challenged, "You've heard of kung fu? Get ready for pork chop!"

"Hold it, now, hey! You don't understand.

These are my friends!" Woody protested.

"Yeah, we're his friends," I agreed.

Then Woody said, "Well, not you." He pointed at the Western toys. "Them."

Just then, another Buzz stepped out of the vent. Now there were two Buzzes-the one with us and this dirty, grimy toy. I was very confused!

The grimy Buzz solved the puzzle by lifting his foot. **ANDY** was written on the bottom of his boot. Now that I really looked, I could see the difference.

The real Buzz grabbed Woody. "You're in

danger here. We need to leave now."

"Al's selling you to a toy museum in Japan," I added.

"I know." Woody pulled free of Buzz's grasp. "It's okay. I actually want to go."

"What? Are you crazy?" Mr. Potato Head said.

Woody explained that he was a rare Sheriff Woody doll and the strange, Western toys were his "Roundup Gang." *Woody's Roundup* was a great old TV show, and he was the star!

"Stop this nonsense and let's go!" Buzz said. But Woody

refused! He said he couldn't abandon the Roundup toys. Without him, the Woody's Roundup set would be incomplete and they'd go back into storage forever.

"You are a toy!" Buzz shouted. "You are not a collector's item. You are a child's plaything! We need to be there when Andy needs us. You taught me that. That's why we came all this way to rescue you."

"Well, you wasted your time," Woody

said. His mind was made up. Then Buzz said, "Let's go, everyone."

"But Andy's coming home tonight!" I cried.

"Then we better make sure we're there waiting for him," Buzz said.

"I don't have a choice, Buzz," Woody shouted. "This museum is my only chance."

"To do what, Woody? Watch children from behind glass?" Buzz called back. He closed the grate.

Chapter Six

The Scary Shaft

Suddenly Woody lifted the grate! "Wait! I'm coming with you!"

He'd changed his mind! "I'll be back in just a second," he said. He wanted to get the other *Woody's Roundup* toys to join us. But the Prospector was determined to go to

the museum. He
screwed the grate
back on the wall!

Woody couldn't
open it. We tried
to help, too.
But the grate
wouldn't budge.

Just then, Al came home! At the sound of
his keys jangling in the lock, Woody and
the Roundup toys ran back to their special
packing case.

He packed up the toys and hurried out.
"Quick! To the elevator!" Buzz commanded.
We all clattered down the air duct behind him.

The elevator rose into view. Standing atop
the car was the dark, ominous figure
that had defeated me in so many games—
Emperor Zurg!

We were trapped! "Watch out! He's got an

ion blaster!" I warned. Zurg fired ion balls at New Buzz.

The gleaming Space Ranger leaped into action.

While New Buzz and the evil emperor struggled, the elevator started to sink.

Our Buzz said, "Quick! Get on!" He found a hatch that opened into the elevator.

But New Buzz was losing to Zurg!

I couldn't look! I turned around and my tail swung behind me, knocking Zurg off balance. He rolled to the edge of the elevator and into the darkness below.

"I did it! I finally defeated Zurg!" I shouted.

We all dropped down to the floor of the elevator, only to see Al going through the big glass front door. Just in the nick of time,

Mr. Potato Head threw his hat and propped open the door.

But Al got in his car and drove off! "How are we going to save Woody now?" I wondered.

Mr. Potato Head spied a Pizza Planet truck idling by the curb. "Pizza, anyone?" I couldn't believe he was hungry at a time like this. But Buzz knew what Mr. Potato Head meant. He rushed us to the truck. Three little aliens hung from the rearview mirror.

Buzz took charge. "Slink, take the pedals! Rex, you navigate! Hamm and Potato, operate the levers and knobs." All the while he talked, Buzz stacked pizza boxes until he could reach the steering wheel. I climbed up to get a good view out the front windshield.

Slinky pushed the gas pedal, but the truck didn't move. Buzz was frustrated. "Why won't it go?"

The little aliens pointed to the stick shift. "Use the wand of power," they droned.

Mr. Potato Head got the car in gear. We followed Al all the way to the air- port.

We screeched to a halt in the parking lot. "There he is!" Buzz pointed into the terminal.

Al stood at the ticket counter. We hid inside a pet carrier to sneak into the baggage check line. We followed Al's case onto a conveyor belt and into the luggage area.

"We need to find that case," Buzz said grimly.

Oh, no! There were two bags that looked like Al's.

The belt dipped down like a roller coaster and we fell. The pet carrier burst open and

we were scattered among the luggage.

Buzz split up the group so we could check both identical cases.

The one I caught up with was full of camera equipment. Buzz and Slinky found the right case. We saw Buzz run along the conveyor belt and open the box. "Okay, Woody. Let's go!" Buzz said.

But the Prospector popped up like a jack-in-the-box and punched Buzz. "Take that, space toy!" he said.

"No one does that to my friend!" Woody yelled. He wrestled with the Prospector. But the wily old fella slashed at Woody with his plastic pick. He tore Woody's arm again.

"Your choice, Woody. You can go to Japan

together or in pieces!"
the Prospector threat-
ened.

"Never!" Woody
said.

"Fine!" The
Prospector raised his
pick for a final blow.

FLASH! FLASH! FLASH! The Prospector
covered his eyes.

We used camera flashes to blind the
Prospector so Buzz could tackle him. "Fools!
Children will destroy you!" the Prospector
ranted.

"I think it's time you learned the true
meaning of playtime," Woody said. "Right
over there, guys."

"No! You can't do this to me!" the
Prospector moaned.

We put him in a child's backpack. From

the looks of the
dolls inside, he
was in for a
wild ride.
But our
troubles weren't
over. "We can't get Jessie out!" Hamm
yelled.

"Woody, help!" she cried

The case was grabbed by a baggage handler.
He threw the box on a tram and drove off
across the runway, where a jet waited.

Woody whistled and Bullseye the horse
slid beneath him. Buzz jumped on behind
and they galloped off to the rescue.

I wasn't there to see it, but Woody and
Buzz together bravely rescued Jessie, just
in time!

Chapter Seven

Safe at Home

T hings were back to normal in Andy's room. The neighbors were all excited about the airport luggage tram mysteriously parked in front of the Davis house. But they soon forgot about it once it was towed away.

Woody was back. Andy fixed his arm.
Not as neatly as the toy collector, but with
loving care.

Andy thought his mom had given him
the new toys, Jessie and Bullseye. He started
playing with them right away. He even
wrote his name on Jessie's boot and
Bullseye's hooves.

"Yee-haw, we're part of a family again!"
Jessie cheered.

A TV commercial came on the screen.
Al stood there in his chicken suit, crying

and selling everything he had for a
buck-buck-buck. Thanks to his greed, he
was broke-broke-broke.

"Crime doesn't pay!" Hamm said.

Life sure was good!